David Grimstone

illustrated by Nigel Baines

*Hodder
Children's
Books*

A division of Hachette Children's Books

First published in Great Britain in 2012
by Hodder Children's Books

1

A Catalogue record for this book is available from the British Library

ISBN 978 1 444 90340 9

Typeset and designed by Nigel Baines

Print and bound by CPI Group (UK) Ltd, Croydon, CR0 4YY

The paper and board used in this paperback by Hodder Children's Books
are natural recyclable products made from wood grown in sustainable forests.
The manufacturing processes conform to the environmental regulations
of the country of origin.

Hodder Children's Books
a division of Hachette Children's Books
338 Euston Road, London NW1 3BH
An Hachette UK company
www.hachette.co.uk

This book is dedicated to Ed's best friend,

Ross 'Chunks' Foster.

It's also for the members of the *Mortlake Massive*:

Callum Pennington, Ashley Irving, Dermott Boylan,

Amy Bennett and Evan Lambert.

REASON... TO HATE MONDAY:

It sucks.

My name is Ed Bagley – and I'm dead meat.
Literally. You could go outside right now,
root through a rubbish bin and find fish
corpses that look better than me.

Next to you, Bagley, I feel fantastic!

You may think you're ugly, or that you smell, or that you're having a really bad hair day. Well, get over it.

I'm uglier.

I'm smellier.

And I'm having a bad hair life ... except that I'm not actually alive any more.

Walking. Corpse.

That's right, I'm a zombie – an unearthly freak in a mad, bad world of blood-sucking, flesh-eating critters from hell.

Only, it's not a complete nightmare for everyone – oh, no. Vampires are drop-dead gorgeous (see what I did there?), werewolves are all emotion and fury, ghosts are stylish with beautiful singing voices, and ghouls don't care what they munch on as long as it smells better than their own feet.

But zombies are a different kettle of

stinking tuna.

Here's the download on my current problems in five points, so even you thicker kids can understand it:

- I stink like your grandma's toe cheese.
- My fat keeps falling off in lumps.
- I'm going to end up like the skeleton hanging in your science teacher's classroom.
- All my friends hate me.
- Did I mention I stink?

That about covers it. For those of you who've followed my hideous, depressing story from the beginning, I don't need to tell you how much trouble I'm in right now. For the rest of you, here's the quickest catch-up in the history of books:

Born.

Lived.

Hit by a truck.

Died.

Woke up a zombie.

Hope that fills in some of the blanks for you. If not, I'm really sorry about that.

No, wait ... I'm over it.

9

I've got my own problems, and they're far worse than yours.

Let's go back to number four on that list: all my friends hate me.

They didn't before, but they do now. I used to boast two of the best friends a walking corpse could hope to have. Then I did something really pants-wettingly crazy and lost them both for ever.

I killed someone – someone they both loved and respected. Someone even I loved and respected.

His name was Evil Clive and, like me, he was a zombie – but he was probably the nicest, most caring dead guy I ever met.

Before I evicted him, that is.

Eviction: that's death for the undead. No one (not even the ghosts, the ghouls and the phantoms) knows what happens when a soul is evicted from its undead shell. I'm not in any hurry to find out, myself. I've died once – I don't fancy dying twice.

Of course, I didn't mean to evict Clive.

His murder was actually the work of my evil left arm.

Er ... I told you about that, right? OMG, I didn't. Right, here goes:

I was normal.

Left arm was normal.

Left arm got possessed by the demonic spirit of Kambo Cheapteeth.

I died, came back as a zombie.

Left arm decided we were growing apart and went out on its own like a talented drummer in a really naff rock band.

However, it tried to kill me first.

A lot.

REASON...
TO FEAR
MY HAND:

It's the Devil's Work

Apparently, no one in the undead community knew when the cell was built, or who it was built for. All anyone knew for sure was that it was there and that knowledge alone was bad enough.

Of course, there have always been tunnels under Mortlake. There are tunnels under pretty much every town in England: sewer tunnels, wartime tunnels, old train tunnels.

Mortlake has all three. Beneath the town there are air-raid runs and the sewers. Below the sewers, there is the abandoned underground. And – deeper still – there is something called the Well.

The Well is basically a giant vertical drop with stairs that snake down around the outside. At the bottom is a single long, dank tunnel that runs to a door so well fortified that it might as well be made of the rock that surrounds it.

And behind that door ...

... was me.

I sat in the darkness, my face streaked wet with grime and the tracks of my tears, wondering if my life could actually get any worse.

Of course, I'd had the odd visitor. Max and Jemini, my former best friends, had both been down to see me at various times – but the conversation was always a bit awkward. If you want my honest opinion, I don't think either of them trusted me anymore and who could blame them? I was surprised anyone bothered to come and see me at all.

CLUNK.

Talk of the devil.

CLUNK.

CLUNK.

CLUNK.

The irregular and nearly deafening sound of the bolts sliding back signalled either a visitor or lunch.

Sure enough, the door yawned open and in stalked Max Moon, the werewolf.

Typically, my oldest and foremost friend in the world of the undead didn't look me directly in the eye, choosing instead to focus on a point about three centimetres over my forehead. I couldn't tell if this was because my jawbone was now completely bare of the tattered flesh that covered the rest of my face, or because he just couldn't bring himself to really lock eyes with such a mindless, moronic loser.

'Hey, Ed,' he muttered. 'Er ... I've brought you some news from town.'

I looked up at him and sniffed a bit. 'Good news or bad news?'

'It's more like – bad and worse. Sorry, mate, but it's mostly grim.'

Max smiled weakly, but there was no humour in it. I guess he felt as wretched about the whole situation as I did.

'There's a big movement of hard-line Clive supporters who want to kill you for what happened. They've got a lot of ghouls, werewolves and vampires working for them, too. They're at war with the council over it, and the whole thing's turning really violent.'

'Awesome,' I muttered, looking down at the floor. 'I guess it's no more than I deserve. Anything else?'

Max swallowed a few times, and I knew whatever was coming was going to be bad.

'Yeah, kinda. The under-council had a meeting, and they've decided to do an ancient test to find out whether your arm killed Clive or you did.'

'Right.' I sniffed miserably and shuffled back against the wall, wincing as some of my exposed backbone brushed the rock. 'I've never passed a test in my life, Max.'

The werewolf shrugged and folded his arms.

'Well, if you fail this test, they're going to banish you from Mortlake.'

'And if I pass?'

'If you pass, they're going to do something much worse ...'

'Well that's just gr— What? Say that last bit again.'

I dragged myself to my feet and tried to make such a disgusting face that Max had no choice but to make eye contact with me. 'Are you sure you haven't got those two punishments the wrong way round?'

The werewolf looked at the floor and

shook his head, just as Jemini sidled into view behind him.

'What's she doing here?' I asked, wishing my voice didn't sound so whiney in the gloom.

The great door slammed shut again, locked from the outside by one of the countless haters I'd gathered following my destruction of the town leader.

'It's like this, Ed,' Jemini said, moving forward, her tearful eyes making me wish she wasn't looking directly at me. 'Either you killed Clive or the devil killed Clive through you. If it's the first case, you're no longer welcome in town. But if it's the second, well, that's really, really bad ... even by your standards. You'd just be too dangerous to—'

'Wait a minute!' I shouted, trying to ignore the fact that my evil left hand

was already twitching like an angry snake.
'Can't I fight this? I mean, him?'

Max gawped at me. 'The devil? Are
you nuts?'

I stepped forward and resisted the
urge to snatch hold of Max's fur with my
good hand.

'Listen,' I snapped. 'I've been run
over, ripped open, smashed through a
wall, bitten, cursed and killed. Right now,

I'd fight the devil and his entire army for what's been done to me. I'm frightened of nothing and no one. I just want all my friends back – because I'd rather be rat food than live in a place where people think I evicted Clive on purpose.'

I half stomped, half slid into the far corner of the room and collapsed into a miserable, defiant heap.

Jemini cleared her throat. 'At least if you let them do the test, everyone will know you weren't in control. I really think we should tell the council that—'

'Tell them to bring it on,' I roared. 'Whatever test they want, whenever they want. I don't care.'

As my tears welled up, I curled into a ball in the corner of the room and hid my face in the crook of my increasingly bare elbow. I didn't look up again until the door had opened and shut, and I was left alone in the darkness with my own despair.

REASON...
TO AVOID
CHEESE:

It's mad, bad and dangerous to chase.

The test finally happened at what I guessed was about mid-afternoon the following day.

The bolts on the great door slid back as usual, but then there was silence.

Complete silence.

Like someone who has just entered a room to find everyone staring at them with weird smirks on their faces, I moved very cautiously, expecting some horrible event to occur at any moment.

This is the test, I thought. Expect brutality.

I reached the door unharmed and put an ear to the door (which turned out to be a mistake when I pulled away and the ear actually stayed stuck on the metal). There was an incredible lack of noise from the corridor beyond.

Nothing.

Slowly, carefully, I grasped the single iron handle on the great portal – and pulled.

Crreeeeeaaaaak.

The door swung towards me as I took several steps back – and there it was: a cold, empty passage filled with dark, gloomy shadows and only the distant flicker of torchlight.

The walls were slimy and covered in moss, the ceiling was crawling with weird insects (including something that looked like three eyeballs joined to a toe) and the floor was ... er ...

I looked down at the floor and did a doubletake.

Then I shook my head.

I even blinked to make sure I wasn't imagining things.

Nope.

There on the floor of the passage was a thick wedge of cheese attached to some sort of metal wire.

'Is this a joke?' I called out, nudging the cheese with my shoe. It moved a bit, but not much. 'What's the test? To see if I try to eat it?'

There was no reply and I looked down again.

The wire pulled tight and the cheese shifted about four centimetres.

I didn't quite know what to do, so I called out again.

'This is ridiculous! What can this possibly pro—'

My hand twitched – not much, but slightly.

The cheese shifted suddenly – about fifty centimetres this time.

My hand sprang out, clawed at the mossy wall and dragged me forward. I used my other hand to slow my progress, but when I looked back the cheese was once again on the move.

'What the hell is—'

I punched myself in the face. It wasn't that hard, but I wasn't expecting it. The blow smashed my crumbling nose and almost knocked me over.

Screaming in anger, I rallied back and gave my left arm such a slap that even the elbow flushed red.

Then the cheese went nuts. It must

have been pulled so hard on the wire that
it actually took off into the air, flying away
from me like a weird, cheddar-version of
Superman.

My evil appendage backhanded me
for good measure, and then dug into the
moss, dragging me along like a little kid
pulls a new kite. I was ramming into walls,
tripping over rocks, colliding with unseen

trees growing from the path.

And, all the while, I'm thinking: this is mental.

The cheese shot up the spiralling steps of the Well, and I went after it. I couldn't help picturing a massive mousetrap waiting at the end of the wire to signal a hefty goodbye to what was left of my crumbling body.

Over the last few weeks, I'd really begun to understand the intense, arcane power of my rogue arm. As difficult as it was to believe that some of my fingers actually belonged to the devil himself, the strength with which I was dragged through the tunnel certainly made it seem like powerful magic was propelling me.

'Argghh!' I screamed as my head glanced off yet another rock, and then I was out – emerging from the top of the well into the dank, glistening tunnels of the sub-sewer.

I couldn't even see the cheese anymore; it was a distant memory.

Then it happened.

Crossing from the sub-sewer into one of the old underground tunnels, my demonic arm swung me around the bend with such force that my head smacked sharply off an ancient brick outcrop and I was immediately knocked unconscious.

I had one very quick and unusual dream where I was riding an elephant with chronic diarrhoea through a garden of enormous vegetables. Then I woke up ...

... and soon wished I hadn't.

My head was still bouncing off something, and I was still being propelled along the ground. But now I felt a cool carpet of grass passing underneath me. Somehow, my loss of consciousness had seen me through three different sets of underground tunnels and now I was back above ground, heading for – what?

I managed to glance up just in time to see the grim outline of Mortlake church against the background of a dark, night sky.

I could now see the cheese flying towards it, the wire dragging it so fast that it actually sprang up in places, ricocheting off rocks and losing parts of its mass in bushes and hedgerows along the way.

It wasn't even cheese-shaped any more. It closely resembled a slightly weatherbeaten block of butter.

I risked another glimpse forward, thinking at first that the entrance to the church was actually wreathed in flame. In fact, the flames were from torches carried by a large group of cloaked and hooded figures that gathered in a rough semicircle on the church steps. A little way behind them, and slightly off to one side, stood Max Moon and Jemini, both looking as worried as I felt.

Flames, said my ever-annoying subconscious. They're going to burn you.

But seriously, what could I do? I quickly assessed my options. I came up with:

- Dig my good hand into the grass and get it ripped off.
- Dig my good hand *and* my legs into the grass and get them all ripped off.
- Dig my good hand and my legs into the grass, stop my progress, have a massive fight with my other hand – lose – and get ripped apart.
- Dig my good hand and my legs into the grass, stop my progress, have a massive fight with my other hand – win – and get burned alive by the town torch-bearers.
- Wait and see what happens.

Guess which one I went for?

Trying to block out the weird chanting that I could now hear ringing clearly from the fast-approaching church entrance, I drew in a breath, thought of my friends and prepared to take one for the team.

I could never have predicted what happened next ...

Screaming, rolling and scraping to a halt, I found myself in the middle of the half-circle of mysterious chanters. I tried to read the expression on Max's face as my rogue hand dragged me to a standstill before the now-stationary cheddar-ball. The chanting stopped, and I noticed one of the cloaked figures at the edge of the semicircle letting go of the handle of a giant winch that must have been retracting the cheese-wire.

I held my breath. My demonic hand suddenly sprang up like a cobra, hovering over the cheese almost as if it was in a sort of bizarre trance induced by really odd flute music.

It poised itself ready to strike and then, to my astonishment, proceeded to smash the cheese into oblivion. I mean, seriously smacking and punching that poor little ball until it had obliterated any sign of it, even to the point where it scratched at the last tiny smears on the church gravel.

I gulped back a confused, nervous glob of sicky phlegm that felt like it might explode from my throat, and my hand relaxed, falling limp as if it had simply gone for a nap after a hard day's work.

One by one, all the hoods in the semicircle were drawn back, revealing many faces I recognized from Mortlake's undead community and a few that I definitely didn't.

While most of the group shuffled back, a tall, thin and rather gaunt figure with sunken cheeks and horrible squint stepped forward.

'Edward Robert Bagley,' he began, and I knew it wasn't going to be good news because at that point I spotted Jemini tearing up and Max trying to comfort her. 'You have been found guilty of being possessed by none other than the father of lies and evil destruction – the Satanic devil himself! And now, your sentence—'

The group suddenly went into a quick huddle, accompanied by a lot of muttering and some very uncomfortable backward glances from the outer members.

Max was looking at me with a sad (but at least slightly supportive) grin, while Jemini had joined in the huddle and was arguing with the man I now thought of as Gaunt. I managed to catch the odd word, like 'Edam' and 'seriously?' but, apart from that, I just couldn't tell what was happening.

I looked down at my cursed hand and noticed for the first time that four of the fingers – *the* four fingers – were now considerably longer than the rest. They'd even grown elongated nails that tapered into points.

'Right,' said a voice, and I looked up again.

Gaunt was now standing apart from the rest of the group, who had obviously come to a unanimous decision over my future.

'Edward Robert Bagley—'

'My middle name isn't Robert—'

'Shut up.'

'Sorry.'

'Ed Bagley – You Will Henceforth Be Taken From This Place And Flown To The Wilberforce Needlepinch Cheese Factory, Where His Satanic Foulness, The Devil Himself, Will Be Drawn From You In What Will Very Likely Become A Pitched Battle To The Death. You Will Be Accompanied By Mr Moon And Miss Jemini, Who Have Taken A Blood Oath To Swear That Justice Will Be Done. Now – What Say You?'

I looked from Gaunt to Max and Jemini, and back again.

'Er . . . thanks?' I managed.

REASON...
NOT TO FIGHT
WITH THE
UNDEAD:

They've got nothing to lose.

We stood on Inchfield Airstrip, a stretch of tarmac beside a really small hangar on the outskirts of Mortlake. I'd never seen a plane take off or land on the runway even when I was alive, so I found it hard to believe that the undead had some sort of regular flight-plan going on. However, I found *a lot* difficult to believe these days, and Max Moon wasn't helping.

'It's like Superman with kryptonite, or water for the Wicked Witch in *The*

Wizard of Oz,' he went on. 'For the devil, it's—'

'Cheese?'

'Yeah. Big time.'

I glared at him. 'That's the most ridiculous thing I've ever heard in my life. For one thing, kryptonite makes Superman really weak, whereas my hand smashed that cheese-ball into the stratosphere.'

Jemini patted my shoulder and gave it a bit of a squeeze, causing a slightly awkward moment when one lump of flesh came away in her hand while another bit slapped wetly on to the tarmac.

'It's true, Ed,' she said, rubbing her hands together and pretending to be cold when she actually just wanted to make sure she wasn't still holding some of my shoulder. 'The devil really, really hates cheese. It's like the bane of his existence.

One little piece – no problem, he can destroy it. But in a factory full of cheese? He'd go crazy. And he might just come to the rescue of his missing fingers. I'm telling you, Ed – the devil absolutely cannot stand to be around cheese.'

'It doesn't make any sense, though! Why?'

'No one really knows. It's a piece of ancient knowledge passed down among the elders of the undead community.'

As the three of us stood there, slightly apart from the town council members, waiting for the plane to arrive, I tried to figure things out.

'So what you're saying is that all those people who go to church and pray on a Sunday should actually be praying at the cheese counter in the supermarket?'

Max sighed and nodded. 'That's pretty much the size of it, mate,' he said.

I turned to roll my eyes at him – and that's when I saw the flames among the trees.

There had to be twenty or thirty of them, all walking with a grim determination. Only a few carried torches – and I assumed they were not werewolves or vampires, considering the danger fire held for both groups. I could also see ghouls emerging from the undergrowth on the edge of the airfield, some scrambling like the fat babies beneath the graveyard, some walking upright like little imitations of children. All in all, it was a truly terrifying sight. Evil Clive's most solid support group had come out in force – and I couldn't really say that I blamed them.

The council stepped in front of us, their cloaks billowing in the evening breeze.

'Let me talk to them,' I said, regretting the words almost as soon as they'd spilled from my lips. 'After all, it's me they want.'

The council leader I still thought of as Gaunt peered back at me twice before returning his attention to the treeline. 'If you absolutely insist,' was all he said, and the group parted slightly to allow me forward.

Max blocked my path.

'Don't do it, mate,' he muttered. 'They'll rip you apart.'

'He's right,' Jemini echoed. 'These people still believe you evicted Clive on purpose, and no amount of arcane testing or basic common sense will convince them otherwise. They'll stop at nothing to see you— Ed!'

I ignored the cries from my friends and marched determinedly across the tarmac. The army of darkness met me about halfway from the treeline, and a single thuggish-looking vampire stepped forward.

'You killed Evil Clive,' he said simply.

I nodded, but looked him straight in

the eye. 'I didn't mean to. The devil has taken control of my hand.'

There were a series of mutterings between the members of the dark army, but the vampire shrugged.

'Either way, you're rotten to the core and we don't want you in Mortlake. You must be destroyed.'

This time, I didn't nod or shake my head or even flinch. 'The council have made their decision. Now, please – go home. I don't want anyone else to get hurt and, trust me, you will get hurt.'

I looked along the line of vampires, werewolves, ghouls and worse, noting several creatures I hadn't even seen at the town

hall meeting. The basic body format of the undead community seemed to consist mostly of claws, fangs and ghostly faces – but I'd also seen the odd freak of nature thrown into the bargain. One of the dark crew even looked like a mini Eater.

I shuddered, but managed to hold my ground.

'I'm going to face my punishment. I am really sorry about what happened to Clive. I know you might not believe me, but he was my friend too,' I finished.

The vampire watched as I turned and walked at an even pace back towards the plane. Every part of me wanted to break into a run, but a voice deep inside my mind told me that everything was going to be OK.

I strode up to Gaunt and managed a weak smile.

'I think that went well.'

The sallow-faced council leader glanced past me and said simply, 'Get on the plane,' but Max and Jemini were already grabbing my arms and propelling me forward.

Then all hell broke loose.

REASON...
NOT TO FLY
UNDEAD
AIRWAYS:

The name speaks for itself.

'What plane? It hasn't even—'

I turned and saw something shimmering on the airstrip in front of me. It looked like the offspring of a massive oblong coffin with wheels and a small plane, but it constantly flickered in and out of focus, as if it had only half a wing in real space.

I didn't have time to argue. As the army of hardcore Clive supporters poured through the trees, the plane door was flung

open and a big, happy-looking Captain
Birdseye dude was standing in the opening,
beckoning us all inside. He had a pair of
empty eye-sockets, but apart from that
the whole scene would have made a nice
TV advert.

I scrambled up the single step that had slid down from the doorway and nearly fell as I climbed inside. Max and Jemini almost rolled over me.

'Welcome aboard,' said the captain, cheerily. 'Just the three of you, is there? Jolly good, I'll get us up and started.'

He turned and sauntered off towards the front of the plane, flickering slightly as if he was in some sort of weird distortion of time.

'Arghghgh!'

Max and I both spun around to see Jemini literally crawling with ghouls. There were two attached to her arms, two on her legs and one latched on to her midriff, all fastening their tiny teeth on any exposed flesh they could find.

The crowd of Clive supporters were attacking.

Max dashed over to help her, but was driven back by a vampire and a werewolf, who both cannoned into him and sent him sprawling on to a row of seats.

'The door!' Jemini cried out. 'Get the door!'

I cast a glance sideways and, before two more werewolves could dive through the hatch on to the plane, I immediately sprang into the access way and pulled the door shut, driving the lock down with all my might.

I briefly considered peering out of the hatch window and making a face at them, when the vampire who'd attacked Max snatched hold of my head and rammed it into the edge of one of the seats.

He looked moderately surprised when he realized that the rest of my body was still standing behind him.

Moving sharply, I bit his hand while instructing my corpse to give him a damn good kick in the back.

He spun around, letting go of my head in order to suck his wounded hand (either because he wanted to stop the blood flow or just because he was thirsty – I couldn't tell which).

My decapitated skull rolled off the seat and on to the floor, and I was just congratulating myself on my killer moves when the plane took off ...

... and my head began to roll.

The deadplane hurtled down the runway at what felt like two hundred and sixty miles an hour. From the outside, I don't doubt it looked like the world's most sleek and sophisticated way to travel – but inside, a lot of really bad stuff was happening.

Max furred-up and punched the werewolf he was fighting so hard that a tuft of hair flew out of its face. The creature staggered slightly and shoved Max into a secured control panel on the wall of the plane.

'Can we just talk about this?' he yelled.

The werewolf snarled again and followed up the assault with a savage punch, but Max dodged aside and the furry fist went slamming into the control panel, shattering the glass that protected a long lever just below it.

Jemini was still screaming, but at least now she was fighting back. She shrugged off three ghouls and made a determined attack on another two, dropkicking one across the plane like a football while digging her fangs into the other as if it was the first course at a really good restaurant.

The ghouls immediately rallied. Scrambling around the plane like hungry spiders, they launched an attack on Max, helping his feral opponent no end.

When he finally hit the floor, the other werewolf ripped off the shattered cover of the control panel behind him and yanked on the lever.

The back of the plane began to open up in a wide yawn, and I noticed for the first time that my head was rolling towards the opening like a golf-ball heading for the green ...

'Arghgh! Help yourself!' I yelled, but my body was a bit tied up with the vampire, who now had me in a Russian Death Grip – about the only wrestling move it's possible to do on an opponent who hasn't got a head.

I was in big trouble, even by my standards.

'Helllllllllp!'

Jemini shrugged off the ghoul she'd been biting and hurtled for the aisle. But she ran too fast and ended up dropkicking my head further towards the yawning touchline.

I rolled nose-over-cheek down the expanse, screaming like a five-year-old girl who's had her dolly pinched.

'Ed!' Jemini put on a final burst of

speed and dived over my escaping skull, using her last precious second to snatch hold of the back seat and reach out with her free hand.

I was seized from the wide and spiralling void of sky. Literally. I even felt the rush of wind on my face and saw the distant specs of figures fighting on the airfield below ...

... and then I fainted.

A cascade of stars danced in front of my eyes and the world swam away. I had a strange and vivid dream about Mortlake, where the living and the undead all mingled together, as if one community was a beautiful painting and the other was a different picture on tracing paper which had simply been placed over the top. Both just walked around, living their various lives without ever knowing of the other community so close to them. It kind of made me sad, but not for long – because I woke up with a bang.

REASON...
NOT TO
WAKE UP:

Things might be even worse.

You've seen it in a million films. The brave hero gets into a really grim situation, then passes out and either wakes up in hospital with lots of caring nurses tending to their wounds or on a feather bed in some magical elf kingdom surrounded by midgets.

I lost consciousness as a decapitated head held in the hand of a screaming she-vampire at the tail-end of a plane twisting through a vortex of rushing air. And then I woke up as a decapitated head held in the hand of a screaming she-vampire at the tail-end of a plane twisting through a vortex of rushing air.

That's right, folks – I fainted for about eight seconds. Can anyone else say 'pathetic'?

Jemini was still clinging to the last seat on the plane for dear death, while Max was taking on all five ghouls and the werewolf he'd been fighting in the first place.

Naturally, he was losing.

Time for action.

'Throw me!' I screamed at the top of my voice, hoping Jemini could hear me above the raging wind.

'What?' came a distorted but frantic reply.

'THROW ME!'

'At who?'

'The werewolf!'

'Are you crazy?'

'Max is in big trouble! Throw to kill!'

Jemini managed to drag herself round until she was clinging to the plane seat like a baby monkey clamped to its mother. Then she reeled back with her free arm and threw, pitched, hurled my decapitated head at the werewolf.

CRACK.

Getting a head butt is painful even when the person delivering the strike is about ten centimetres away from you.

Getting a head butt from thirty feet, well, that's kind of difficult to describe. It scores about a ten on the Painometer. At least, it did for wolf-boy. He flew back as if he'd been hit by a torpedo, smacked into the control panel and slid down the wall with a gurgle. He must have caught the lever, too because the back of the plane was slowly beginning to close up again.

'Max!' I screamed, bouncing off a row of seats and mashing my nose in a collision with one of the little square windows. 'Get the ghouls out! Quick! Qui—'

My words were stifled as I rolled off the headrest and bumped on to the floor.

Still partially dazed from his bitter scrap with the rival wolf, Max had to use a chair to drag himself off his feet. Now fully wolfed up, he looked like a big carpet with teeth.

'Ghouls!' I reminded him. 'Ghouls!' It was then that I suddenly realized why my stomach hurt so much when I didn't actually have a stomach connected to my brain. I squinted towards the cabin end of the aisle and saw my body being punched in the stomach by fang-boy.

Max Moon knew how painful ghoul-bites could be – and he wasn't taking any chances. Leaping from seat to seat, he snatched up each fat baby and, as if he was handling hot coals, flung them down the aisle like some lunatic bowler at a ten pin alley. One by one, the ghouls were disappearing into the fast-shrinking airstream with a variety of mad, cackling cries of panic.

I reached out with my mind and finally made mental contact with my detached body. Fighting for control, I closed my eyes and imagined twisting out of the vampire's grip and dropkicking him towards the back of the plane.

I opened my eyes – and couldn't help but feel a little disappointed.

The good news was that my body had twisted out of the vampire's grip.

The bad news was that I was now punching the stuffing out of one of the plane seats while my opponent took a moment to get his breath and snigger behind my back.

I gritted my teeth and tried again.

This time, my body met the vampire's attack with a sharp elbow that sprang up and caught him square on the jawline and sent him crashing to the floor.

Ha! He wasn't expecting that.

Max Moon was nearing the last level of what had quickly become the National Ghoul-tossing Challenge. With a final, thunderous bellow of rage he hurled the last fat baby at the thin sliver of daylight that still remained visible between the closing jaws of the plane's tail-end.

The body was sucked through the gap, and the last thing anyone saw was a chubby little face with a vaguely contorted expression.

I can't stand ghouls.

When the tail closed, Jemini let go of the back seat and collapsed in a heap.

'Argh!'

The cry came from Max, who was going toe-to-toe with the incensed werewolf. Incredibly, it had recovered from my awesome head butt and was lifting Max over his shoulders, preparing to deliver some sort of airborne powerslam.

Jemini rolled on to her feet and flew down the aisle like a swooping eagle, landing on the werewolf in a fury of vampiric fangs and claws. The wolf dropped Max and the three of them rolled away into one corner of the plane, looking like a cartoon fight ball with arms and legs appearing and disappearing at random.

I was concentrating on other things. Using every tiny section of mind power I could summon, I ordered, instructed, commanded my body to come and fetch my head.

It spun around, delivered two quick

punches that actually winded the vampire – and began to stagger quickly in my direction.

There was a brief moment of terror as one of my own feet nearly stamped off my nose, and then I was lifted carefully on to my shoulders.

I concentrated hard until the soft, wet, sickly sucking sound indicated that I was re-attached.

Now it was stomping time.

I spun around just as the vampire careered into me, but two swift knee lifts had him thinking twice. I snatched hold of his throat with my demonic hand, hoping it would do something pretty awesome of its own accord.

It didn't.

The vampire looked down at the clasp, realized there wasn't much behind it and broke the hold, scooping me up like a rag doll and tossing me aside.

I hit the wall of the plane and fell awkwardly between two rows of seats, groaning as three of my fingers rolled under one of them.

Jemini leaped on to the vampire's back, sinking her fangs into his neck and ripping great clumps of his hair out in fistfuls.

Screaming with rage, the vampire threw himself back and tried to ram her against the wall, but Jemini was too quick for him. She evaded the strike and slammed the side of her hand into the vampire's throat.

It clawed ineffectually at the sudden exhalation of breath, and collapsed into unconsciousness. Jemini fell on to her knees beside it, shaking her head to steady herself.

'Good move!' I cried, still hunting around on the floor for my fingers.

Max ducked two strikes from the werewolf and gauged a vicious wound in its side. Then he snatched hold of the wolf's face and dragged it down, driving his kneecap into its forehead.

It twitched a few times and then fell into a deep, dark slumber.

Max and Jemini both clambered to their feet, while I used the plane seats to haul myself into a vaguely upright position.

The plane looked as though a bomb had gone off inside it.

To my astonishment, as the three of us fought to gain some sort of composure, the cabin door opened and the captain strode out with a pleasant and somewhat detached smile on his face.

'Thank you for flying with us, today,' he said, opening his arms widely and pointing in all directions. 'The exits are here and here. Under your seats, you will find a safety vest which you can inflate by blowing into the small tube at the top. Once again, thank you for flying Deadspace Airlines.'

He beamed at us one last smile and headed back into the cockpit, closing the cabin door gently behind him.

I turned to look at Jemini and Max, who were also covered in blood. 'What is wrong with that guy?'

Max shrugged. 'He's on a loop. That's what deadspace is – it just goes round and round. Just be grateful you didn't become a phantom ...'

Grateful.

I looked down at myself and grimaced.

'I'm not grateful for having the devil's fingers! What's the point of having an ultra-powerful, demonic hand that only fights when it wants to?'

I slumped into one of the seats, curled up against the wall and prayed for sleep.

REASON...
NOT TO FLY
DEADSPACE
AIRLINES:

They don't stop.

When I woke up this time, all was calm and peaceful. It's a pity I was stuck to the leather of the seat by a smelly glue that seemed to consist largely of my own spit, but you can't have everything.

The deadplane was hurtling along at breakneck speed, but it was also making practically no noise. For some reason, that fact really unnerved me. However, it was nothing compared to my stressful conversation with Jemini.

'Say that again?' I gasped. 'What do you mean, we're not landing?' I was looking out of the window on to a thick carpet of forest that rushed past below us at an impossible speed. 'We're just above the treeline: we have to be landing.'

'This plane only takes off and lands at Inchfield,' Jemini explained. 'Apart from that, it goes in a circle around the world.

It's like a video that just keeps on playing – we're lucky it's even solid enough to fly in, really ...'

I didn't want to guess what she meant by that, so I just nodded. 'So how do we get off?'

'We jump.'

'What? We're going at two hundred miles an hour or something!'

'Oh, get over it, Ed,' Max laughed. 'Seriously, it's such a rush! I'll just crash through the trees, Jemini will fly to the ground and—'

'I'll fall to pieces?'

'Well, yeah ... but only like you always do. Besides, you'll put yourself back together again.'

'Don't worry, Ed,' Jemini said, giving me another of her mini-squeezes, 'we're right behind you.'

Max made a face that indicated he was about to do something crazy and bolted over to the plane doors.

'Max—'

'You only die once, Ed ...' he cackled, sliding down the lock and throwing open the portal so that a whirlwind blast of air almost ripped it off the plane.

Then he was gone.

Yep – the big furball jumped. Just like that.

I turned to make some sort of stunned remark to Jemini, but she rose into the air and blasted after him.

If you don't jump now, said the niggling little voice in my head, they'll be MILES away by the time you land.

I gulped back a tiny piece of vomit that had risen in my throat, closed my eyes, and ran straight into the wall next to the open doorway.

'Owww! Damn it!'

I staggered back, holding my nose, and got sucked through the hole anyway ...

'Aaaaaaaaaaaaarggghhhhh!'

Some people say you haven't lived until you've jumped out of a plane and seen the earth screaming towards you a million billion miles an hour.

I hate those people.

REASON...
NOT TO LAND
IN A FOREST
FACE-FIRST:

It hurts.

The air hit me like a tidal wave of pure, chaotic energy.

My hand snapped back and flew off into the wind.

I gritted my teeth, waiting for my head to rip apart from my neck and follow it. Thankfully, this time it stayed put, unlike my right leg, my left ear, at least half of the body fat on my belly, and something I didn't even realize I had until it exploded out of my mouth and shot away.

I would have sobbed, I would have

cried, I would have yelled out in total misery and despair if I hadn't crashed through the forest roof at that point.

I swear to this day that I hit every single branch of the massive, ugly, rotten tree I landed in. But the absolutely worst thing that happened to me during my whole afterlife happened as I hit the lowest branch: a twig went straight through my right eye and it popped like a fat spot.

My head snapped back with the pain and a sickness came rushing over me. I wriggled off the branch and fell about twenty feet, half splashing, half thumping into a dirty puddle at the foot of the tree.

I yelped and rolled over, forgetting that I had a leg missing, and trying but failing to stand on the remaining one.

Cursing everything I could think of, I glanced up to see my eyeball stuck on the end of the lowest branch like a cherry on a stick.

'Are you OK, mate?'

The voice was unmistakably Max's, and I squirmed around to face him.

'Do I look OK?' I snapped, getting even angrier when it became apparent that Max was completely unscathed apart from a sparse covering of leaves and other forest foliage. 'I mean, seriously – no leg, no good hand, half my flesh missing, and my former eyeball wedged up there.' I pointed with one of my non-devil fingers. 'Would you be OK?'

Jemini appeared from between two trees a little way down the path. If anything, she was even less dishevelled than Max.

'Clive could see quite well with two empty sockets,' she said, with a shrug. 'Are you sure you actually need your eyes?'

I was about to hurl a raft of abuse back at her when I tried closing my left eye tightly and realized that I could actually see quite clearly from the empty socket. If anything, the world was in slightly sharper focus, but in a very fine blue haze.

However, it's the principle of the thing.

'I know it's greedy,' I muttered, 'but I

really would like my other eyeball back – so if you can both just hang there for a second, I'll lie down here and concentrate on remote-calling all my missing body parts, thank you so very much.'

REASON...
TO RUN FROM
LOUD NOISES IN
THE FOREST:

Everything in there
wants to eat your face.

A heavy rain was soaking through the trees
as we squelched along the forest path. In
fact, squelched wasn't really what we were
doing at all. We were all running as if the
hounds of hell were after us. For all I knew,
they were.

A series of loud and terrifyingly
pitched howls had erupted all over the
forest and, the way I looked at it, if a
werewolf and a vampire suddenly both

broke into a run, it's probably a fair bet the thing behind you doesn't do weekend shifts at Disney World.

Still, I was feeling slightly better. Despite the fact that Jemini told me my body reforming was the most disgusting thing she'd ever seen, my mood was actually beginning to pick up. Sure, I'd made enemies in Mortlake, but at least I hadn't been banished by the council. When it came right down to it, I had a chance to fight the devil in a cheese factory, which – according to Max – was like a team of Jungle Warriors playing Manchester United in the Amazon basin.

'Where are we, anyway?' I said, trying not to sound as happy as I felt.

'Germany,' Max growled, ringing some rainwater from his fur. 'We're just crossing the border from France. The cheese factory is about two minutes away.'

'The Wilberforce Needlepinch Cheese Factory,' Jemini corrected him.

We trudged on through the rain.

'Who is Wilberforce Needlepinch, anyway?'

Jemini and Max shared one of those glances that reminded me they'd both been undead a lot longer than I had.

'He was just an old guy who owned the factory,' Max muttered. 'He died a long time ago.'

I nodded and waited a few seconds to let the pair of them relax. Then I grinned and said, 'So why did you just look at each other in that weird, freaked-out way?'

Jemini sighed.

'Well, let's just say that Kambo Cheapteeth wasn't the only man ever to do a deal with the devil. Needlepinch was another one who went down that path, and when he died – something horrible happened to him, something that only happens to people who did some really bad stuff during their lives.'

'What was that?'

'He became a Host.'

I waited for more information, but both Max and Jemini were shuddering.

'I'm guessing you don't mean like a game-show host?'

'A Host is a person whose soul gets imprisoned and transformed at the same time.'

'Imprisoned and transformed into what?'

The rain was getting heavier now and we found ourselves slipping and sliding through the trees on a sort of downward slalom. When we had finally all crashed, skidded and staggered from the edge of the forest, Jemini stuck up her hand and pointed with a single, shaking finger.

'Into that,' she finished.

Max and I both gulped.

There, on a low hill beside the edge of the forest, was the ugliest, most sprawling

and impossibly massive building I had
ever seen in my life. Its many spiny turrets,
buttresses and crenellations made it look
like a massive, spiky-haired face, while
the hundreds of shattered windows
reminded me of row upon row of gnarled,
jagged teeth.

'So,' I said, trying to keep my voice steady, 'what you're saying is that the Wilberforce Needlepinch Cheese Factory is actually ... Wilberforce Needlepinch himself.'

As if to illustrate the point, a streak of lightning suddenly lit up the entire expanse of countryside.

I was about to point out how eerie it made the building look when a second bolt hit me directly on the forehead, frying my skin like a side of streaky bacon ...

Max leaped ten feet into the air.

Jemini screamed.

I just smiled faintly and fell over backwards.

REASON...
NOT TO GET
HIT BY
LIGHTNING:

It hurts.

Since I'd joined the elite but kinda crummy membership of the walking, talking dead, physical pain had become second nature to me.

If you poke me in the eye, it doesn't really hurt – it just stings, smarts and squelches a bit.

If you pull my arm off, it doesn't really hurt – it just burns like a demon and aches all to hell.

Being scratched, torn and ripped

apart by tiny flying imps was a complete bummer, I have to admit.

But being electrocuted and burned, flayed and melted by a whacking great bolt of pure energy was still right up there at number one.

I screamed so hard my lungs felt like they were going to explode. Max rolled me up and down the hillside and Jemini – for reasons best known to herself – kicked me in the face a few times (to 'stamp out the flames,' she said).

When I finally staggered back to my feet, I felt like an ant squashed on the bottom of a giant's shoe and I looked like a pork scratching.

'Argghhghh – the pain!'

'Breathe, Ed!'

'Yeah, mate – just breathe!'

'Ahhhhhhh!'

I held my breath and tried to wish away the agony. It seemed to work ... and within a few seconds we were all up and walking again, heading for the great looming evil that was the factory.

The rain poured on – and the conversation was just as depressing.

'Does it look really bad?' I asked, trying to ignore the smell of fried chicken.

'No, mate.'

'Not at all, Ed – you look fine. Ha! I'd still go out with you on a date ...'

I glanced sideways at her, but she was doing a good job of not sniggering.

Max whistled between his teeth. 'Seriously, mate. We wouldn't lie to you. It's not that bad. Personally, though, I'd steer away from mirrors for the time being.'

And that's when I knew the truth. I could have gone on a double date with a girl made entirely of elephant snot and she would have been the looker.

If the Wilberforce Needlepinch Cheese Factory looked ugly from a distance, up close it was a real eyesore. The front doors were hanging off their hinges, both covered in some weird algae that had also mutated much of the brickwork on either side.

It was truly a hideous sight but I had no real choice but to go in. Otherwise, where could I go? The world of the newly undead was alien to me. Sure, I could return to a mob of haters in Mortlake ... But what if I went back a hero? A zombie who'd fought the devil and won? After all, if I didn't win I didn't have to worry about going anywhere ever again.

Besides, Jemini and Max had taken a blood oath to ensure that justice would be done. Whatever that meant. I was just really lucky I had friends willing – quite literally – to put their necks on the line to support me.

Gulp.

I returned my attention to

Wilberforce Needlepinch's grim creation.

There were no lights inside the building and leaves swirled up around the entrance, whipped by some sort of minor vortex that nestled inside the main passage. To finish off the grizzly picture, it seemed as if half of the actual building was missing, demolished perhaps by a fighter plane during the war or even by some natural disaster.

Looking at the monstrosity, there was only one statement I felt inclined to make.

'Who'd buy cheese from here? Even a deranged mouse with no sense of smell would bang past it at a hundred miles an hour ...'

Jemini rolled her eyes. 'How many times do we have to go through this, Ed? We interact with the spirit of buildings – that's why you never see kids in Mortlake

School or people in the high street. I can
assure you that it doesn't look like this to the
breathers. It is a working factory. There's
enough cheese in there to kill a mouse the
size of a dinosaur.'

I nodded reluctantly and we ventured
up the stairs, beyond the giant entrance
doors and into the main hall.

If the undead really did see only
the souls of buildings, then Wilberforce

Needlepinch had been rotten to the core. His cheese factory was completely mank-tastic.

Now, here's a fact: cheese smells. I'm not talking about your auntie's ear-cheese, either – I'm talking about the normal, everyday stuff. If you leave cheese on a kitchen worktop long enough, it will actually follow you to work in the morning.

The Wilberforce Needlepinch Cheese Factory stank to hell and back.

The corridor yawned widely ahead of us and an eerie, chittering sound was now clearly audible in the gloom.

Something was crawling on the walls. At first, I took it for a shadow or the wind bothering the moss, but now, as we moved on down the hall, I could see there was definitely a carpet of tiny, odd misshaped insects trailing our progress. They moved in a bizarre formation, almost like an arranged attack unit, zigzagging through the myriad network of cracks in the wall pattern.

'Hate this place already,' Max muttered.

I shuddered in agreement.

The three of us arrived at a T-junction, and we instinctively looked to Jemini for guidance.

'Which way?'

'I'm not sure,' she said, sniffing the air. 'But the smell of cheese is strongest that way.'

We turned right and headed down a new corridor with whitewashed walls and a creepy, tiled floor that reflected our own images back at us. I don't know what surprised me more – that Jemini had a reflection or that this part of the floor was clean enough to see it in.

At another T-junction, we all turned left – and stopped dead.

The new corridor was a dead end, but the blocking wall contained an enormous painting lit by a strange and unnaturally pale light.

The picture was of a short but very fat old man in what looked like a doctor's lab coat. He had sagging jowls and a greenish

tinge to his skin, and he wore a pair of tiny, circular spectacles. The picture was odd, and something about the way the old man was gleefully rubbing his hands together really gave me the creeps. Looking over at Max and Jemini, I could see they felt the same way.

'Wilberforce Needlepinch,' Max muttered. 'Has to be, doesn't it?'

'Let's go back to the junction,' Jemini said, smiling uncomfortably and leading both of us away by the elbows.

All three of us kept looking back.

We soon rounded yet another bend in the endless maze of passages but, this time, the cheese smell grew really strong.

My hand began to twitch.

REASON... NOT TO SUMMON THE DEVIL:

He's the devil.

My hand flew up suddenly and slapped on to the wall like a wet fish hitting a chopping board. Max and Jemini both leaped back as my four demonic fingers dug into the plaster and began to wrench me forward at an alarming rate.

'Arghgh! Here we go again! Argghhh!' I cried.

I was dragged up the corridor, catapulted through a set of swing doors that looked as though they should have been guarding a casualty unit at the hospital, and driven headfirst down a new passageway that, to me, smelled more of disinfectant than cheese.

'Help me! Arghgh! Hold me back or something! Help! HELP!'

I managed to throw myself on to the floor and wedged both feet against the wall so that my rogue limb was forced to pull my entire weight forward.

It did. Despite straining every muscle and sinew in my rapidly decomposing body, I couldn't stop myself slowly inching away once again.

'Max!' I screamed at the top of my lungs. 'Jemini! Where are you two?'

I twisted around on the floor, trying to see between my own legs as I was hauled off towards the far end of the corridor.

Max and Jemini were both following

me, but neither was in any particular rush. In fact, Max looked like he was taking an early afternoon stroll in an old lady's garden!

'Help! What's wrong with you?'

Max shrugged his shoulders.

'We can't, mate,' he called out. 'It's the rules of the council. You've got to do this on your own. I kno—'

'Sorry, Ed,' Jemini interrupted. 'We can only intervene once the demon is out of the box, so to speak. Good luck, though!'

Good luck? Was she kidding!

My demonic limb was now firmly in control, spinning me around on the tiled floor and rushing me towards yet another set of heavy swing doors at the end of the passage.

I smashed open the doors like a human-sized battering-ram and flipped over twice before skidding, scrambling and sliding to a standstill in a room twice the size of a cathedral.

Max and Jemini spilled into the vast chamber behind me, both primed and ready for some sort of explosive confrontation.

My hand was now going nova, the four fingers twitching, scratching and even snapping at the other five in some sort of spider-like duel.

But at least I wasn't still being pulled along the corridors. And suddenly I saw why.

The columns I had taken to be rows and rows of pillars holding up the ceiling of the room were actually stacks of cheese. They rose higher than the surrounding walls which I could now see were also blocks of cheese piled in miniature obelisks all along the back half of the room.

The place smelled baaaaad.

My hand snapped back and forth, rising up like a cobra and slowly turning three hundred and sixty degrees as it felt the incredible presence of so much dairy goodness.

Then it happened.

First my hand punched the floor, driving me on to my knees and slamming the fist down ...

Once.

Twice.

Three times.

Then there was a sickening, severing, scorching sound and a tiny line of blood ripped across the knuckles between the back of my hand and the four possessed fingers.

'Argghh!' I screamed, clutching at the hand and holding it down as blood and bone began to defuse.

The fingers twisted and turned as they scrambled to escape, leaving torn and jagged wounds behind them.

And then, heaving back on my hand with a spitting hiss at the escaping digits, I

watched helplessly as the fingers shot across
the floor like insane worms towards the
biggest cheese stack.

'You're free of him, Ed!' Jemini cried
from just inside the doorway, with Max
baying behind her.

'Run, mate! Run!'

I turned tail and tried to flee, but a

dark and terrible cackle echoed around the vast room. The swing doors slammed shut and a network of moss immediately grew over the join.

'Do you really think it would be that easy?' said a loud, menacing voice like thick syrup. 'Did you truly believe that you could trespass on my property without a reckoning?'

To this day, I really wish I hadn't looked up. I still don't know why I did. I guess something in the corner of my vision told me things weren't right.

Very close to the ceiling of the immense hall, a network of ventilation grids provided a fresh flow of air to the cheese-makers.

Today they were providing a new tide of the weird insects I'd seen in the entrance corridor. They swept out of the grid and

swarmed across the ceiling, moving in one
long, bleeding shadow that made it look
as though an impossibly dark cloud was
passing overhead.

I swallowed back a gulp of fear and
spun around, determined to find another
way out of the room.

Unfortunately, I ran into big trouble.
The four finger worms had made a beeline
for the largest tower of cheese and had
burrowed straight into it, bringing the

entire stack down on top of them. The debris of so much fresh cheese was too much for the fingers to take, so they had shot back out of the pile and were writhing weakly on a tiny cheese-free scrap of floor at the end of the hall.

'Stamp on them, mate!' Max yelled, his attention split between the hunt for an escape route and the trillion insects advancing overhead.

'Leave it, Ed!' The counter-warning

came from Jemini, who had overtaken the pair of us and was throwing big lumps of cheese off a table she'd decided might be blocking the route to freedom.

I really wanted to leave those fingers alone, honestly, I did. But the memory of what they made me do to Evil Clive rose inside my head and I just couldn't help myself.

Screaming with rage, I took a run up and leaped into the air, landing with a half-skid among the finger worms.

'Take this, you stubby little freaks!' I screamed, stomping and stamping every square inch of the ground while the pudgy digits snaked and slithered around my boots. And then, a massive, thunderous avalanche of sound exploded behind me.

'The wall!' Max boomed. 'The wall is moving! Look!'

Sure enough, one entire side of the room was crunching forward, crushing tables, chairs and a mountain of cheese on its path towards us. Worse still, a series of bizarre cracks and holes had scarred the surface of the wall, turning it into a warped and twisted face that I just knew belonged to the reckless soul of Wilberforce Needlepinch.

'Ed! Eddddd!' Jemini had finished heaving aside blocks of the cheese, but was now staring wide-eyed in my direction.

I gawped at her.

'What is it? What's wron—'

A flash of green whooshed beneath my feet and slowly I turned around.

The four fingers had knitted together across a strip of thin flesh that was, very slowly, growing a large and demonic-looking crimson hand.

The devil.

I took several steps back ...

... crashed into Max ...

... and the insects began to
rain down upon us.

REASON...
TO HATE
INSECTS:

**They have more legs than teeth,
and that's just wrong**.

All hell was breaking loose – and I mean that
quite literally.

Max and I were rolling around on
the floor, clawing at our own faces and
spitting out great mouthfuls of the teaming,
streaming mass of shiny black insects. The
chittering critters were everywhere. I was
scooping them out of my nose, my ears and
even my eye-sockets.

If anything, the attack on Max was
worse. I couldn't even see my friend any
more. He was just a great big furry cocoon,

wrapped in tiny, shiny, black shells.

The wall continued to rumble, crushing everything in its path and rapidly shrinking the room.

Jemini rose quickly into the air, soaring towards us at her top speed.

Fangs and claws elongating, she reached down and slashed two swathes of the insects out of Max's fur. She took hold of the remaining down in her fists and rose into the air, pulling Max up with her.

'Shake yourself, Max! C'mon! All dogs can do that!'

Max wriggled around inside the swarm, slowly shedding shower after shower of the insects on to the factory floor.

I vomited up a throatful of insects and yelled out for help.

Jemini quickly zoomed to my rescue, but she never made it.

A massive clawed hand, gleaming red and wreathed in flame, snatched her out of the air and hurled her against the wall as if she was a puppy's chew-toy. She hit the brickwork and plummeted to the ground.

There was a grim rumble of earsplitting laughter, and the hand swept back towards me.

I wriggled and squirmed in the wild mass of insects, spinning myself around on the floor and trying desperately to bite down on anything crunchy that ventured beyond my lips, but I had other problems ...

The devil's hand closed around my legs and hauled me into the air, shaking me free of the insects and holding me upside down over the shrinking expanse of the great cheese hall.

Seeing the devil for the first time is a truly sobering experience. I'll be honest, though, seeing him upside down wasn't actually that bad. I think I would have been a lot more terrified had he held me the right way up.

He bellowed like the demented roar of

a mountain lion and I gagged as he blasted me with the most revolting breath I'd ever smelled. I might have even thrown up a little in my mouth.

'ED ... BAGLEY,' came the booming voice.

I caught an image of charred, burning skin, missing tufts of hair and melted visage – then realized that there was a mirror on the moving wall of the factory and I was actually looking at a reflection of myself. As I watched, the reflection changed – and I saw Evil Clive.

Then it happened. Suddenly, the factory, the grim shadow hanging over me, even my friends, all disappeared ...

I was sitting in a white room on a really comfortable sofa. Sitting opposite me, on an equally fluffy red armchair, was Evil Clive. He was exactly the way I remembered

him, right down to the fell grin and the
backwards Dead Donkey baseball cap.

I gulped. 'C-Clive?'

The skeleton nodded. 'Hey, Ed.
How's it going?'

'F-fine,' I managed. 'I-I'm dreaming,
right?'

'Yes, you are.'

'Did I die?'

'No ... you fainted. Don't feel bad about that. You've just seen the devil in the flesh and your mind can't cope with it. But you know what they say? Anything that doesn't kill us, makes us stronger.'

I nodded, slowly, taking in the general whiteness of my surroundings.

I gulped again. 'Er, will I be going back soon?'

'Yes,' said Clive, with a friendly nod. 'And when you do, remember this: nothing is ever as bad as it looks. OK?'

I smiled, weakly. 'Yeah. OK.'

'Good lad. Off you go, then.'

I felt the room begin to swim around me. I guess I was waking up.

'C-Clive!' I shouted, into the receding glimmer of the dream.

'Yeah?'

'I'm sorry about ... evicting you.'

The skeleton's grin loomed out of the blinding light, and the voice behind it, muttered, 'Kid – don't sweat the small stuff.'

I awoke, cold and sharp.

Fighting to see my real surroundings, I craned my neck up again, and immediately wished I hadn't.

The devil was massive.

I'm going to say that again, just so you understand properly.

The devil was massive, and I'm not talking about the size of that big kid in Year 12 who keeps getting sent to detention for beating up the teachers. I'm talking two-storey house massive.

If you've ever seen films or documentaries about the Greek myths, then you'll know what a Minotaur looks like: a great hulking bull on two legs with muscles rippling through every limb. The devil is basically a very big version of that. The horns weren't entirely unexpected, but I'd always thought they would point up, not down. The nose-ring was a shock, because I never realized the devil would keep up with fashion and stuff.

Still, you get the picture.

Monster.

'ED ... BAGLEY,' he said again.

I tried to stop choking and snivelling long enough to see what was happening in the room.

The wall had stopped rolling forward and was now extending rows of sharp spikes from every join in the brickwork. Evidently, Wilberforce Needlepinch was going to make damn sure his infernal master's chosen victims weren't going to escape anytime soon ...

I twisted and tried to kick out of the devil's grip, but he lifted me even higher. Now I was face to face with the jaws of doom, and the smell was indescribable.

'You dare to challenge me, Ed Bagley? Me – who could crush you in a heartbeat?'

The world turned upside down once again and I found myself held the right way up in the devil's fist. I couldn't move.

Revealed in all its glory, the face of the beast was truly terrifying to behold, and I could actually feel the flaming yellow eyes burning what remained of the skin on my face.

'You destroyed Kambo Cheapteeth, one of my very favourites – and even the sacrifice of that skeletal loser you slaughtered cannot make up for that.'

'You did that through me!' I managed.

I gritted my teeth and tried to pour every ounce of strength into my arm muscles, but the grip was like iron.

'And now, Ed Bagley, your own time has finally come. Prepare to be destroyed.'

The pain started as a dull throb, regular but all over my body in small bursts, a low, burning ache that slowly intensified. I looked down and saw flames begin to

spring from between the giant fingers. I was
on fire ... I was going to burn into dust.

Max sprang to his feet and charged,
digging his claws into the devil's chunky
red legs and taking a big, enormous, savage
werewolf bite.

The devil flinched and kicked out, smashing Max through the side wall of the factory. He landed on a hillside in the pouring rain, and I could just about make him out trying and failing to get back to his feet.

That's when the hopeless set in, and I stopped struggling to free myself from the grip still pinning me to the wall. A kind of weary haze tumbled over me and I closed my tired eyes.

This is the devil. What chance can we possibly have of surviving ...

Jemini had shaken off her insect coat and was back in action. Grabbing a heavy wooden leg off a half-destroyed table, she was now battering away at the struts supporting one of the giant cheese vats at the back of the room.

CRUNCH.

The vat gave a monstrous, creaking sigh and hit the tiles with a bang, spewing soft, molten cheese across the factory floor. The dairy river rolled over all the floor cracks and quickly became a tide of cheesy goodness.

Jemini staggered back from the vat, bleeding and exhausted, but very pleased with herself.

The devil screamed, and twitched, waking me from my defeated, dreamy state. The great beast's cloven-hooved feet were now covered in an ocean of sticky cheese and had begun to smoke and hiss. I squirmed, wriggled, shimmied and snaked my way under the fingers and dropped, tumbling head over heels, into the splashing river of molten cheese.

The devil bellowed with rage and ripped his hoofs free from the sticky mass.

I hit the surface of what was now basically a cheese 'n' insect soup and flipped myself on to my back, just in time to dodge the massive hoof that came slamming down centimetres from where I'd just landed. I dodged right, scrambled to my feet, and leaped sideways.

The hoof came down again like a crack of thunder, but this time it split the tiles and splashed cheese and insects in every direction. It would have flattened me like a pancake if I'd still been lying there.

'Out!' I screamed at Jemini, who was still fighting to get to her feet through the sticky cheese soup that covered the floor. 'Out!'

Then I turned and bolted for the

hole in the wall that Max had been hurled through.

The devil charged after me.

'Arrghghh!'

I slipped in the goo, landed flatly on my side and gagged. The cheese stank to the depths of hell and back.

'Go, Ed! Go!'

Jemini had flown in front of the devil and was clawing ineffectually at his enormous face while he tried to swat her away like a bluebottle.

Following her instructions, I span on my heel and ran like the wind, or at least like the wind would run if it had the devil after it.

I leapfrogged a medium-sized mountain of packaged cheese and made for the whole. As I ran, Wilberforce Needlepinch decided to head me off at the pass, driving his spiked wall forward with incredible force.

'Arghghghnnnnoooooooooooooo!'

The scream came from Jemini, who'd been snatched up and hurled by the devil. She rocketed over my head and disappeared through the hole, bouncing over the hillside in a weird episode of fits and bursts.

Please let her be OK, I thought. She's only here because of me. I guess at least she was out of the factory.

That's when a last-minute plan occurred to me. A plan so mental that even a half-deranged mutant elephant wouldn't have tried it.

That didn't stop me.

I skidded on the river of cheese and surfed my way in a complete arc until I was face to face with the devil once more. I shot forward, running with everything I had and

flattened myself
out and slid
between the red
giant's two great
legs.

Then, amid
the beast's sudden
confusion, I greeted
the onrushing wall
of spikes with open
arms, took hold of two
of them and began to

climb. Blood sprayed from my rotting hands as I progressed up the moving wall, yelping in pain as the spikes bit into me. When I reached the middle of the wall, I must have looked like a chicken staked out on a griddle.

Partly astonished and partly bemused, the devil turned this way and that, peering all around the factory floor before he thought to cast a glance up at the shifting wall.

135

'Yeah,' I cried, screaming out the word with every burst of breath I still had in me, 'here I am, you hoof-trottered, hairy-legged, cow-headed moron.'

The devil's eyes gleamed with sudden fire.

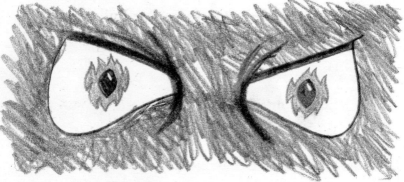

'You dare to—'

'Yes I dare! No wonder you live down in hell, you great ugly monster! I've seen dog turds that scrub up better than you!'

'You will d—'

'Even your horns are straight from Naff City, you moose-faced sack of dried camel vomit!'

'Argghghh!' The devil boomed, shaking the foundations of the factory. 'ROAOOOOOOOOOOOOOOOR!'

His hot, stinking breath exploded through my hair and nostrils.

'Is that all you've got, you mud-licking Minotaur wannabe? No wonder Evil Clive scared the hell out of you. What did he do, show you a mirror?'

Now the eyes were blazing like twin furnaces, and every muscle on the bulbous arms was wrestling every vein for control of the explosion of strength that was brewing.

'EDDD ... BAGGGLEY—'

I rolled my eyes.

'Yeah, yeah. Do your worst! Come over here, and I'll kick your stinkin' teeth in!'

The devil charged.

Flames burst from his hoofs with every

step, and it hurtled towards me with all of its spite and anger, rage pouring from every orifice and spit flying from the corners of its stench-ridden mouth.

As if detecting what I was about to do, the soul of Wilberforce Needlepinch desperately tried to stop the wall from moving forward, inching back with what must have been phenomenal mental effort.

Sadly, it was too little too late.

I jumped down and slid forward beneath the devil's legs, and span around to watch it crash into the wall of deadly spikes.

The soul of Wilberforce Needlepinch cried out in warning.

'Arghghghghgghghghghghghgh!'

There was a sickening thud, a squelching sound and an eye-watering waft of stink ...

And then there was silence.

I staggered to my feet, dragged myself forward and half stumbled, half fell over the pile of packaged cheese that barred my way to the hole in the side of the factory wall. Then, putting in as much of a determined effort as I could muster, I began very slowly to ascend the mountain. I tumbled back every few steps, but that didn't stop me and I persevered, hauling my devastated body towards the gap and my freedom.

Finally, reaching the edge of the hole, I looked out on to the rainy hillside, just able to make out the two bedraggled shapes that were my two best friends, and a tired smile split my cracked and shattered lips.

I'd made it. I had finally defeated the devil and—

'ED BAGLEY.'

I turned around – and, this time, I very nearly cried.

REASON... NEVER TO COUNT THE DEVIL OUT:

Didn't you hear me last time? He's the devil!

A shimmer of greenish, golden energy was bleeding from the giant creature speared to the factory wall. A separate, arcane strand of the same magic was seeping from the wall itself – and both were meeting in the middle.

I was so, so tired of fighting. I actually didn't think I had any more strength left to give. I wanted to run, but something about the weaving lines of energy grabbed my attention and simply wouldn't let go.

I gulped.

The two pulsing colours melted together and began to form into two separate humanoid shapes. One was squat and round, the other tall and thin. One had flabby jowls and tiny, circular spectacles, the other swept, jet-black hair and a triangular goatee beard.

I took a deep breath as the shapes completed their transmogrification.

A series of grim cackles filled the room, but these seemed to come from the very walls – either that or from the millions of tiny, chittering insects that littered the floor, all drowning in a lake of melted cheese.

The two figures on the factory floor were now clearly defined and very visible. One was unmistakably Wilberforce Needlepinch. The other, I had to assume, was the human manifestation of the devil himself.

I took a deep breath and bunched both my fists into balls.

'Wow,' I said loudly, looking down on the both from my lofty perch. 'I admit I'm shocked. I really didn't think you two could get any uglier ...'

Then I turned around.

And I really, really, really ran.

REASON...
TO RUNAWAY
FROM A SECOND
FIGHT WITH
THE DEVIL:

You're just not listening, are you?

I felt like Indiana Jones in the first part of the Raiders movie. I was running towards Max and Jemini waving my arms and they were jumping up and down with glee because they thought everything was fine.

It was only when I got close enough for the pair of them to read my tortured expression that they both realized I was still in a heap of trouble.

The rain hammered the hillside, turning every muddy puddle into a deadly patch of quicksand.

'Wh-what is it?' Jemini shouted, as I skidded into her and Max and knocked them both on to their backs.

'He's coming!' I shouted, trying to get my words to make more sense than the garbled, twisted way they came out. 'The devil is coming!'

We all turned back towards the factory, and – sure enough – the devil and Needlepinch were both floating eerily across the grasslands towards us.

'The forest!' Max screamed. 'Let's run for the forest.'

'Why?'

'It beats staying here, mate!'

'Good point!'

We scarpered for the edge of the trees, pausing briefly to wrench Max out of a narrow muddy stream.

'Can the devil cross running water?' Jemini yelled, as we ran on.

'Yeah,' Max shouted back. 'It's witches that can't.'

'Great!'

We reached a thick clearing and all slid to a halt.

'Let's split up,' I said, determinedly. 'You and Jemini go that way. I'll head east.'

'Why?'

'Because the devil is after me, and I'd rather nobody else died on my account. Get it?'

'Got it.'

'Good.'

As Max and Jemini hared away, I bolted off through the trees, bellowing at the top of my voice, 'Over here, you bearded, bony, jackal-toothed monkey-boy!'

My voice echoed through the trees, but sounded weak even to me. I was seriously beginning to run out of decent insults.

The forest was lonely, dark and deep, and I had some truly awesome hiding places to choose from.

So only the gods know why I selected a really obvious-looking bush right in the middle of the first tiny clearing I came across.

Thinking myself really clever for finding such an invisible position, I hunkered down and waited.

And waited.

And waited.

Eventually, after what felt like at least half an hour, I folded back some of the foliage and peered out into the clearing.

That was when a voice beside me said, 'Who exactly are we looking for?'

I jumped out of my skin ...

... and the bush.

REASON...
TO FIGHT FOR
YOUR LIFE:

It's a pretty amazing gift.

The devil strode around the clearing, clicking his fingers and humming quietly to himself.

As he did, the bush sprang up around me and curly tendrils of foliage snaked around my ankles and thighs, rooting me to the spot.

'I don't care what you do to me,' I lied, my voice shaking pathetically in the shadowy clearing. 'I'm just glad my friends got away from you.'

The devil stopped in front of me and raised a bony finger to his lips.

'*Shhh.* Quieten down now, Ed. Your friends will be fine. My associate, Mr Needlepinch, is kindly fetching them for me. I don't think they'll cause him too much trouble. He's a very ... resourceful man.'

I felt the tears rising inside me, a horrible sadness that I just wanted to fight and fight, but I knew I was too weak to go on.

'What do you want from me?' I said wretchedly. 'I mean, I'm dead already.'

The devil grinned. 'Oh, but you could have been so much more, Ed. Just look at Kambo Cheapteeth. Now there was a dark warrior. And then there's you: pathetic, utterly pathetic. I gave you my own fingers and the opportunity to come over to my side and wreak havoc with them. You were only the second person to resist my will in the entire history of civilization. The first—'

'—was Evil Clive.' As I finished the sentence, I just knew it was true.

'Ha! You couldn't beat him, then! He resisted you as well! What did he have, two of your toes? Your manky elbow?'

The devil folded his arms and took a deep breath. Several curls of red smoke filtered down from his pointed nose.

'I'm going to inflict upon you the most savage and brutal punishment I can think of. And then I'm going to send you back to Mortlake.'

I lowered my head and glared at him.

'There's nothing you can do to me which I haven't already—'

'Oh no, Ed, you're quite, quite wrong.'

Max and Jemini appeared on the edge of the clearing. Both were walking in strange, guided steps and both had an odd, faraway look on their face. Needlepinch fell into step behind them.

I swallowed, but my throat was dry. 'Please,' I said, 'I'll do anything, but please don't hurt my friends.'

The devil chuckled.

'No harm will come to them, I can assure you,' he said, a sick, disturbing smile on his face. 'As much as I'd love to evict them both completely, there are rules – even for me.'

Then he cracked his knuckles, took a deep breath, and pointed at Jemini.

A wall of flame shot from the end of his fingertips and completely engulfed her.

'Jemini!' I screamed. 'No! JEMINIIIIII!'

The vampire-girl began to thrash around in a sudden, mad explosion of panic, but the flames just became stronger, turned to a pale shade of orange and intensified.

I closed my eyes and tried to block out the tortured cries of my doomed friend. When I opened them again, Jemini was gone.

I fell to my knees, a grim mixture of desperation, panic and sadness driving me on.

'What have you done to her? What have you done?'

I scrambled to reach the patch of ground where Jemini had been standing, but the weeds and tendrils around the bush held me fast to the ground. I pressed myself away from the dirt and craned my neck until I could see Max's face.

'I'm so sorry, mate,' I sobbed, trying to get the words through my choking throat. 'I'm so sorry.'

But Max simply wasn't there. He stared down at me with nothing more than a morbid, idle curiosity. His face was an empty shell.

The devil cackled smartly and fired a second bolt of flame at Max.

This time I watched through tear-streaked eyes as my best friend in the world of the undead disappeared into fragments of floating air.

I laid on the dirty, mud-soaked ground, awaiting whatever doom was about to be laid upon me. I didn't care any more: my only friends were gone, and nothing else mattered.

I felt the devil's hand clasp my throat and lift me off the ground. I sagged, feeling my charred and devastated flesh hanging loosely on my rotted frame.

'Ed Bagley,' said the devil, holding me aloft, his gleaming eyes piercing what was left of my immortal soul, 'prepare to meet your fate.'

A single tiny flame licked up the arm of the devil, but when it hit my flesh it exploded in a writhing, twisting, molten spew of furious fire.

The devil thrust me back on to my feet and frantically I tore and scratched at my body, trying desperately to hammer out the pain ... to no avail.

Piece by piece and chunk by terrifying chunk my zombie flesh burned, melted and ran away from me, leaving my ivory bones exposed to the moonlight.

A ghostly fire took everything that was left of the skin I'd squeezed spots from, the skin I'd cut and grazed when I'd fallen from my bike, the skin I'd hugged in the cold and stretched in the sunlight ...

... and all that was left was the bones beneath.

As I looked up at my tormentor, I was now nothing more than a human skeleton, a mirror image of Clive: grinning on the outside and sobbing on the inside at the cruelness of my inevitable fate.

But the worst was yet to come ...

The devil clapped his hands, dancing around the clearing with Needlepinch scampering along in his wake. Turning at the edge of the trees, he looked back and gave me a demonic wink.

'Goodbye, Ed Bagley,' he said, with a jovial nod. 'I can't say you weren't fun to work with – but now, I'm afraid, is really not your time. Be grateful. Most people never get to experience this ...'

He pointed at me and the searing, screaming bolt of fire that had taken Max and Jemini slammed into me, reducing my pitiful existence into memory and sorrow. As the flames took the last of my vengeful spirit, I collapsed on to my bony knees ...

REASON...
NOT TO
QUESTION
FATE:

It moves in mysterious ways.

The pain hit me.

A whirl of air slammed into me and I was flying through white light, screaming and thrusting every tiny pocket of strength I possessed into trying to fight the rushing onslaught that swept me back.

Two flashing blurs of energy spun past me and suddenly, in a buzz of strange lightning, Max and Jemini were both just there, each of them holding on to me with arms outstretched, gritted teeth and spit flying from their mouths.

'You're alive!' I shouted. 'You're both alive!'

Max grinned, but his legs had begun to disintegrate behind him. It was like he was being dragged away, one molecule at a time.

'Ed! Hold on!'

I was overcome with a grim sense of despair. 'I can't!' I yelled. 'You two were the best friends I ever had. Do you hear me? Be nice to each other!'

Jemini screamed at me. 'Just don't … let … go!'

Then she too began to dissolve, fragments of her spinning off into the blinding void.

'Jemini!' I shouted, wincing as Max's grip slipped from my other hand.

'Ed!'

'Max!'

Then, just like that, they were gone ...

... and I cried out, collapsing on to tarmac with a yelping, curdled cry that made me sound like a five-year-old girl.

My leg was trapped.

I dropped the few school books that hadn't already fallen out of my arms and tried to twist my ankle out of the grate, but it was held firm between the bars.

That's when I heard the sound. A sound all-too familiar – and getting louder by the second.

A truck. A very, very big truck heading along the road in my direction.

On an evening like tonight, in rain this torrential, the driver probably wouldn't even see me.

I renewed my efforts, scrambling

around like an idiot, frantically pulling at my leg until I felt the blood begin to flow from my ankle.

If I pulled any more, I'd probably lose my foot – and I really didn't want that to happen.

The truck was visible now, slamming along the road at a ridiculous speed.

I was doomed.

Mum always said those truckers were going to kill someone sooner or later – I just never thought it would be me.

'Stop!' I screamed, waving my arms back and forth like a lunatic. 'Stop! Stop! STOPPPPPPPPPPPPPP!'

The rain hurtled down.

Thunder rumbled overhead.

I twisted and turned with my foot trapped firmly in the grate ...

... and the truck rolled on.

I closed my eyes, screaming so much louder than I ever thought my voice could manage, waving my arms in vast, flapping circles while the end of my life raced towards me.

The truck slammed into me like a hundred-pound sledgehammer hitting a slice of bread …

… or it would have done – had the driver not swerved at the last moment and skidded to a noisy, hissing halt in the pouring rain.

My eyes remained tightly shut, my hands slowly dropping to my sides, as I realized two things very quickly.

First, that I wasn't nearly as scared as I probably should have been. And, second, that – amazingly – I was still alive.

The door of the truck's cab swung open and a pair of hefty leather boots hit the tarmac. The driver, a tall man in a long black overcoat, stomped across the road towards me.

'You insane, kid?' he spat. 'I could've killed you!'

I looked up at the driver, allowing my wretched expression and prone position to speak for itself. 'I didn't have much choice,' I said, pointing to my leg.

The stranger nodded and moved around beside me. He reached down and pulled up the grate as if he was lifting a cup of coffee, then gently worked my ankle from between the bars until I'd managed to wriggle free. He even picked up my school books and shuffled them back into my arms.

'Thanks for that,' I said, managing a weak smile. 'Oh, and thanks for not killing me.'

The stranger grinned.

'You should be more careful out here,' he said, reaching into his overcoat and pulling out a battered-looking baseball cap which he thrust on to his head. 'It's raining pretty hard, and if a truck like mine hits you, you're not exactly going to walk away.'

He adjusted the cap until it was facing backwards and gave me a wink. 'Still, you know what they say. Whatever doesn't kill us, makes us stronger. Take it easy.' Then he turned and headed back to the truck.

'Is that your favourite band?' I called after him, pointing to the cap.

The stranger paused, but didn't turn around.

'Dead Donkey?' he said. 'Nah, not really. I just like their merchandise.'

A few seconds later, the truck began to roll away towards the old factory.

'Weird guy,' I muttered.

Then I bundled all the wet school books into my bag and headed for the distant lights of Mortlake.

As I walked along the same road where, just a few days earlier, I'd fought vampires and ghouls, I realized that something important had changed. It wasn't the half-familiar shape of the old town, the creepy way the trees all brushed together as if they were hugging for warmth, or even the pale wash of moonlight over the road. It wasn't the thunderous sound of the trucks starting up at the factory, or the way the wind and rain roared past at a lunatic pace, obliterating practically all sight and sound.

The thing that had changed was the little boy walking determinedly towards his old home.

The thing that had changed was ... me.

I didn't feel scared any more – not of other kids, not of evil clowns, not even of the horrors of Mortlake.

For some reason beyond my understanding, the devil had given me a second chance. Maybe he'd been impressed with my fighting spirit, or even the fact that I refused to abandon my friends. Maybe he just didn't like me and wanted to keep me as far as possible from the lands of the undead.

Whatever the reason, crazy, inept, clumsy Ed Bagley had been given another shot at life.

And, this time, I was determined to live it.

Inside the grizzly mind of David Grimstone

Do you talk to Nigel Baines, the illustrator, about what you want the characters to look like?

Never. I like Nigel's drawings to be a complete surprise. He interprets the books in a way that is completely his own and it's always exciting to see what he comes up with! His illustrations are hilarious.

Do you like scary films and creepy stories?

Yes and no. I love dark, psychological or even supernatural horror, but I always prefer the stuff that's scary without showing too much gore. Films with buckets of blood in them aren't cool: they just put me off my dinner.

If your arm were to be possessed by someone's demonic soul, who's would you choose?

Hmm ... tough one. If I have to choose someone real, I'd go for Mick Jagger because he's got the moves. If I could choose anyone real or fictional, it would be Captain Jack Sparrow because I just KNOW I'd have an awesome time with his soul in the driving seat.

Do you have any tips for someone who wants to be an author?

Write EVERYTHING. Seriously. Write letters, stories, reviews, articles, the lot. Never stop writing. Also, enter every competition you can find and read every book you can your hands on. Especially books written by David Grimstone, because – basically – he's awesome.

What gave you the idea for the Undead Ed books?

My great granddad crawled out of his grave and attacked me with a spade. Er ... no, seriously, I just thought there was too much serious or romantic stuff published about the undead – so I wanted to write a series that made fun of being a zombie. I love Ed as a character because he moans about EVERYTHING just like I do.

Do you think that clowns are evil?

Not really. A clown is just some poor guy trying to do a job – like a postman or a builder. So, no, clowns aren't evil – except Pennywise the dancing clown in Stephen King's book *IT* – he is SERIOUSLY evil.

What would you do if you got lumbered with the devil's fingers?

I'd hold them to ransom and refuse to hand them back unless he gave me eternal life, a massive castle on a hill and Jamie Oliver as my personal cook.

What was your best ever Halloween costume?

It was actually just a black cloak with a plain white mask – I've never seen so many terrified people in my life. I'm still not sure why.

What's your favourite spooky joke?

What did the zombie's friend say when he introduced him to his girlfriend? Eugh ... where did you dig her up from?

What's your favourite part about being an author?

I get to make up stories for thousands of people – what could be better than that?